THE SECRET GAMES OF
MAC **MAXIMUS TODD**

NEW DYSL...
EARLY CHAPTER ...
READING LEVEL GRADES 1-2

W9-CML-142

NOW AVAILABLE IN CANADA AND THE US

What makes these books dyslexia friendly?

Font

This series uses a dyslexia-friendly font called OpenDyslexic. OpenDyslexic is a new open source font created to help with some of the symptoms of dyslexia. Letters have heavy-weighted bottoms to indicate direction and help readers quickly figure out which part of the letter is down, which helps readers from rotating them around. The unique shapes of the letters can help prevent confusion caused by flipping and swapping letters.

This font is being updated continually and improved based on input from dyslexic users. To learn more about OpenDyslexic, visit the website.

Paper stock

These books use cream-coloured paper which is recommended for dyslexic readers instead of white paper. The paper stock is also matte, instead of glossy, and is a heavier stock to prevent any glaring through from the other side of the page.

Layout

The layout of pages in a book is important to dyslexia readers. Both the lines and paragraphs are kept short to avoid dense blocks of text. There is lots of spacing between lines and paragraphs and wide margins and headers are used to break up the text. Hyphenation isn't used for words that aren't usually split, and lines are kept left justified with a ragged edge.

more titles in

The Secret Games of Maximus Todd!

Hyper to the Max

Clever Max invents a game to keep his Super Fidgets at bay for the day. Too bad his arch enemy Mandy Beth discovers what he's up to and tries to trip him up! Will Max win at his secret game?

Frantic Friend Countdown

Max has a dilemma. Everyone's got a best friend except him. But when a new kid arrives at the school, Max plays a secret game to make him Max's buddy. Too bad the new kid would rather hang out with barf-breath Mandy Beth, peskiest pest in the entire town!

Flu Shot Fidgets

Max is at the doctor's office, where the stress of getting a needle sets off his Super Fidgets. Quick-thinking Max invents a secret game to try to stay calm. But Max will have to invite #1 pest, Mandy Beth, over for a play date if he loses.

Big Game

by L. M. Nicodemo

illustrated by Graham Ross

Jitters

Formac Publishing Company Limited
Halifax

Formac Publishing Company Limited recognizes the support of the Province
of Nova Scotia through Film and Creative Industries Nova Scotia. We are
pleased to work in partnership with the Province of Nova Scotia to develop
and promote our creative industries for the benefit of all Nova Scotians. We
acknowledge the support of the Canada Council for the Arts which last year
invested $157 million to bring the arts to Canadians throughout the country.

Cover design: Meghan Collins
Cover image: Graham Ross

Library and Archives Canada Cataloguing in Publication

Nicodemo, L. M., author
        Big game jitters / L.M. Nicodemo ; illustrated by Graham Ross.

(The secret games of Maximus Todd)
ISBN 978-1-4595-0330-4 (pbk.).--ISBN 978-1-4595-0429-5 (bound)

        I. Ross, Graham, 1962-, illustrator   II. Title.

PS8627.I245B53 2016   jC813'.6   C2015-907252-2

Formac Publishing Company Limited   Distributed in the United States by:
5502 Atlantic Street   Lerner Publishing Group
Halifax, Nova Scotia, Canada   1251 Washington Ave N
B3H 1G4   Minneapolis, MN, USA
www.formac.ca   55401

Printed and bound in Canada.

Manufactured by Friesens Corporation in Altona, Manitoba, Canada in
May 2016.

Job #222734

Contents

Chapter One

SOCK TROUBLES

It was early Sunday morning, and Max was in his bedroom searching through the dresser.

"WHERE ARE THEY?"

he mumbled.

He pulled out a drawer and dumped everything onto the floor. **Clonk!** He pushed the pile this way and that. Still he could not find them.

Max raced down the stairs. His mother, Granpops and baby Sarah were in the family room.

"Mom," Max said in a rush,

"WHERE ARE MY SOCKS?"

His mother looked up from her chair. Sarah sat on her lap. On Sarah's lap was a book.

"Which socks?" she asked.

"YOU KNOW,"

Said Max, in an I-can't-believe-
you-don't-know-what-I-am-talking-
about voice. "My lucky Laserman
ones."

"Oh. I've just thrown them in
the washing machine," Mom said.
"You'll have to put on another
pair."

MAX'S EYES GREW ROUND
LIKE TWO PING-PONG BALLS.

"Uh uh!" he cried. "I can't wear
REGULAR socks today."

Granpops put down his
newspaper. "Why not, buddy? One

pair's as good as another."

Max groaned. "It's the championship soccer game today. I HAVE to wear my Laserman socks."

"That's right. I almost forgot."
Granpops rubbed his wrinkled face
and leaned forward. "The key is
to pass, Max. Don't try to run it
up all the time. It'll tire you out."

"Oh Dad," said Max's mother.
"It's a bunch of kids playing a
friendly game of neighbourhood
soccer. Don't make it so
competitive." She turned to Max.
"Just have fun, my guy."

Max covered his face with his
hands.

NO ONE UNDERSTOOD HOW IMPORTANT THE SOCKS WERE.

"We're gonna lose if I don't wear those socks," he muttered. And, of all the games he'd ever played, this was one he could NOT lose.

"Who're you playing against?" asked Granpops.

"Spencer's team," Max said. "They're really good."

"Humph! I don't like that Spencer.

He's one mean kid,"

said Granpops. Mom gave him a you-shouldn't-say-that look.

Max nodded.

SPENCER ViLANE

WAS
mean.

He bullied kids in the schoolyard. He chased the neighbourhood cats. If Spencer Vilane became the soccer champion, it would be like the bad guy winning at the end of a movie.

"See? We can't lose," Max said.

"It'll be fine, Max. It's not the disaster you think it is," said Mom. "It's ONLY a game."

Max rolled his eyes. Sometimes grown-ups didn't get it.

Chapter Two

Laserman to the Rescue

Max slunk back to his room and started pacing. As he paced, he counted out laps.

"One."

ONLY a game? Easy for Mom to say. She won't have to listen

to smelly Spencer brag about
winning all summer long.

"TWO."

This IS a disaster. It's even
worse than the time I got an
eraser stuck up my nose.

"THRee."

Wearing the wrong socks
is BAD luck. We'll lose and
someone'll probably break a leg.

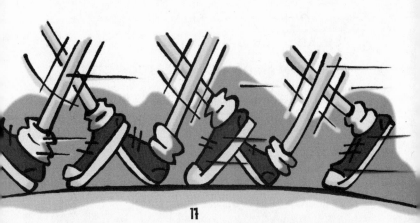

Whirling into the next lap, Max noticed his collection of action figures on the bookshelf. Laserman was in the very front. Max stared at the plastic figurine and suddenly grinned.

He plunked down on the clothes heap. This time he scrounged around for his hockey socks, the long ones that went to his knees. When Max found them, he put them on. Then he grabbed Laserman from the shelf.

"Hope it's okay with you, buddy," he said to the figurine.

Stretching out the sock on his left leg, Max shoved Laserman in. The action figure pressed snugly against his calf.

"Ta-Daaa!

A homemade Laserman sock!"
Max said, pleased with his
invention. "Now I better test it
out."

Imagining that he was in a soccer game, Max jumped up and kicked. Next he jogged in place. After that, he rolled along the floor. No matter how much he moved his leg,

LaseRman WOULD nOT BUDGe.

The doorbell rang and Max ran to answer it. He was expecting his best friend Shiv Pal to come by early to practise.

"Hey, Shiv," Max said as he opened the front door.

Not Shiv. Mandy Beth Bokely. Pesky girl, pesky neighbour and, as if that wasn't enough, pesky soccer-player-on-the-same-team-as-Max.

Max frowned.

"OH. iT'S YOU.
WHAT DO YOU WANT?"

"What do I want?" Mandy Beth screeched. "Maximus Todd! We're gonna play the most important game of our lives and you're asking me what I want?"

She let out a dramatic sigh. "I

came early to see if you wanna
practise before the game. We

REALLY

have to beat Spencer's team."

"Geesh, calm down," he said,
letting her in the house. "It's
ONLY a game."

He peeked down at his Laserman sock. It made him feel better. "Um . . . we can practise in the backyard. Shiv's coming too."

Mandy Beth flipped her long braid. *"Good. I've got a couple ideas on some plays."*

Max Rolled His eyes.

Mandy Beth always had ideas. Annoying ones. And she made Max listen to them, even if he didn't want to.

"It's up to Shiv," reminded Max. "He's captain."

The doorbell rang again and

there was Shiv, standing on the porch with a soccer ball under his arm. "Hey guys. Better practise.

"WE REALLY GOTTA BEAT SPENCER'S TEAM."

"Good idea, Shiv," Max agreed. Mandy Beth's eyebrows shot up, giving Max a that's-exactly-what-I-said look. Max decided to ignore it.

They moved to the backyard and talked about plays. They practised passing and goal kicks. And though no one had ever done a head-butt in a game, they practised that too.

"Keep the ball away from Spencer — *that's all we gotta do*," Shiv said when they were done.

"Sounds impossible," complained Max, running a hand through his curly hair.

"Maybe he'll sleep in and miss the game," offered Mandy Beth, hopefully.

Shiv chuckled. "Maybe he'll get the chicken pox."

"Maybe zombies will surround his house and he won't be able to leave — for the whole summer," laughed Max.

On their way out, Mom handed Max a water jug. Granpops fist-bumped everyone to wish them good luck.

"You sure you don't want me

to come along?" asked Max's grandfather. "I could coach you guys."

"No thanks, Granpops," said Max. "This is a kids-only game. Remember?"

MAX, MANDY BETH AND SHIV HEADED DOWN THE STREET TO THE PARK.

"Have a good time," Mom called out from the front porch.

Behind her, Granpops waved while making a kicking motion to remind Max to pass.

Chapter Three

The Game Begins

By the time they arrived at the park, most of the players were already there. Other kids had come to watch too. Some were carrying posters that read:

"Go Hawks!"

"Hornets Are #1!"

Max spotted spiky-haired, *squinty-eyed* Spencer standing on an old tree stump. His team was gathered around him in a loose huddle.

"WE'RE GONNA DEMOLISH THEM, GUYS,"

Spencer roared. "Let's show 'em that the Hornets are THIS . . . YEAR'S . . . SOCCER . . . CHAAAMMPS!"

"YEAH, YEAH," his

team chanted back.

"Hey, Shiv," Spencer yelled out, "time to set up the goals. Or are the Hawks too chicken to start?

PWaUK,
PWaUK,
PWaUK!"

Max scrunched his face at Shiv, who just shrugged. Grabbing the plastic planters that a player had brought, Shiv met up with Spencer. They paced out the nets and marked them with the planters. Meanwhile, kids started

to arrange themselves on the lawn.

Lori Skenders was the official ref, mostly because she was the only kid with a genuine referee's whistle.

The teams had been made
at the beginning of the season
by everyone drawing cards.
Spencer and Walter "Spitzy"
Spitson played forward for the
Hornets. Deedee Pardo was centre
and Glenna Lin, one of Max's
classmates, was defence. In net
sat Luis Fernandez.

The Hawks' forwards were
Mandy Beth and Shiv. Jorge
Fernandez (Luis's twin brother)
played centre and Tanya
Skenders, Lori's younger sister,
was the goalie.

Max usually played defence.
He wasn't the fastest runner or
the best kicker, but he'd move in

front of any ball to block.

They would play until either
team reached three goals.

"*Get ready to lose!*" Spencer
shouted out at the Hawks.

Max leaned down and rubbed
the side of his sock for luck.

THWEEEET!

Lori blew the whistle, and the championship game began.

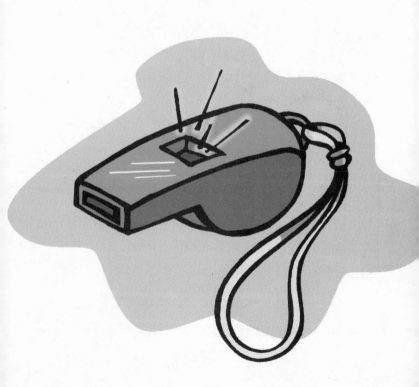

Chapter Four

Kicked Out

In no time, Spencer nabbed the ball. His teammates moved farther downfield, but Spencer didn't pass. Not at all.

BALL HOG, thought Max.

Though he was short and
stocky, Spencer weaved between
players like he was skating on ice.
Not even Mandy Beth could catch
him. Max spied Spencer's mean
grin as he neared, angling for a
goal.

"C'mon Laserman. C'mon
Laserman," Max muttered as he
turned to face Spencer.

Spencer approached fast. He made a fake move to one side and then switched direction. With a loud grunt, he kicked the ball, aiming for the far end of the goal.

Keeping his arms tight against his sides, Max jumped right at the ball.

THONK!

It was the perfect block.
The soccer ball bounced out of
bounds.

"WAY TO GO, MAX!"

His teammates shouted.

Spencer glared. Max smirked
back. Then, because he couldn't
help it, he bent to pat his sock.
"Thanks Laserman," he whispered.

"Hey, what's with your leg?"
Spencer sneered, noticing Max's
bumpy sock.

Max swallowed the sudden
lump in his throat. "Nothing," he
answered, turning away.

"Hang on," Spencer pressed.

His voice rose.

"WHAT'S iN YOUR SOCK?"

The field grew quiet as other players stopped to stare.

"Oh," shrugged Max. "It's just . . . uh . . . Laserman."

Spencer scowled. "Huh? Let me see."

Max leaned down and put his hand into his sock. He grabbed the Laserman figurine and pulled him out.

EVERYONE BURST OUT LAUGHING.

Max's face reddened.

"You are such a WEIRDO!" Spencer scoffed. But then his expression changed.

"Wait a *minute*," he said, "you can't put an action figure in your socks. It isn't fair. It's cheating!"

Shiv stepped forward. "Ah, Spencer. Let him be. It's no big deal."

"Uh uh!

iT iS a BiG DEAL,"

insisted Spencer. "*You never see real soccer players doing that. It isn't allowed.*"

Max stood still. The hand that held Laserman got clammy.

Kids started murmuring:

"Max CHEATED."

"NOT FaiR."

I didn't cheat, thought Max. *Did I?* The figurine was plastic. *It wasn't the real Laserman.* But maybe it

gave off some special power. He'd
made a pretty amazing block.

"Okay, Spencer," said Shiv. He
turned to Max. "How 'bout you
leave Laserman with Lori."

Max nodded. He wanted nothing
more than to have everyone

forget about Laserman and return
to the game.

"Not good enough," said
Spencer. "I want a penalty kick."

EVERYBODY GASPED

Spencer stood with his
hands on his hips, looking like a
concrete wall.

Lori stepped in and called a vote.

Spencer stared down every kid, daring anyone to vote against him. Even Tanya, the Hawks' own goalie, sided with Spencer. In the end, he won seven votes to four.

Set-up was quick. Spencer took a short run and then kicked.

THE BALL WHIZZED EASILY PAST TANYA.

"Ha! Ha! Ha!" Spencer squawked, running around the field with his fists pumping the air.

Now it was 0 – 1 for Spencer's team.

Max hung his head.

iT'S aLL MY FAULT.

Chapter Five

A Visit from the Fidgets

"Everyone back to their positions," called out Lori

THWEEEET!

The game started up again. Only this time, Max found he had trouble paying attention. He didn't have his Laserman socks like he should have. And he didn't have his Laserman figurine — which had been the next best thing.

In his head, Max could hear a noise. Faraway and faint at first, but getting louder. It sounded like the roar of a fast approaching T-Rex.

Without warning his arms became topsy-turvy. And his legs got flubbery-rubbery.

And his insides jumbled up into one big tangle.

"Oh no! I CAN'T believe it!" Max wailed.

THe SUPER FiDGETS!

Once in a while Max would get an extreme case of the jitters. He'd be too hyper. Too restless. Paying attention would be as impossible as a snowstorm in the summertime.

And when that happened, there was only one thing Max could do. He needed a game — something to keep his brain busy on the inside so he could focus on the outside.

Max had to think fast. After all,

He was in the middle of a championship soccer match!

One that his team was losing!

The engine of an overhead plane cut through Max's thoughts.

He looked up. *I know what I'll do! Every time something flies overhead, I'll do ten jumping jacks.*

At once, Max began jumping in place.

And if I don't do the jumping
jacks, I will say in front of
everyone that Spencer Vilane
is the best soccer player in the
whole neighbourhood.

THERE. HIS SECRET GAME WAS SET.

The noise in Max's head started
to slip away. And his legs and
arms felt like his own again.

He glanced behind at Tanya,
who was giving him a very
strange look.

"Oh . . . I needed to exercise a
bit," he called to her. "I wanna be

at the top of my game."

Tanya nodded, but the strange look stayed.

Chapter Six

No Defence

With the Hornets in the lead,
Max's team turned up the heat.
Mandy Beth took possession of
the ball, dodging Spencer and
Deedee. Then she passed it to
Jorge. He flew by Spitzy and ran
it to the far end of the lawn.

"Go! Go!" Max called out.

Glenna, the Hornets' defence, slipped and tumbled, giving Jorge an opening. Closing in on the net, Jorge kicked hard. The ball bounced once and soared past his twin brother Luis's outstretched hands.

"Woohoo! Hawks rule!" several kids cried out. Everyone from Max's team ran up to pat Jorge's back.

Max was going to head over too, but at that moment a yellow butterfly glided by. It fluttered above his head.

"Geesh," he grumped.

He stopped in his tracks and counted out ten jumping jacks.

"ONE . . . TWO . . . THREE . . ."

From downfield, Max noticed Mandy Beth and Shiv stare. In less than a minute they were marching

over. Of all the people Max knew, they were the only ones aware of his secret games. Mandy Beth, because she had forced it out of him long ago. Shiv, because he was Max's best friend. And best friends tell each other secrets.

"DO YOU HAVE THE SUPER FIDGETS?"

Mandy Beth demanded.

"Or," piped in Shiv, "are you stretching to stay loose?"

Max offered a sad smile. Shiv always tried to look on the bright side of things.

"Well . . ." Max began.

Just then Lori called from the
sidelines, "Positions everyone!"

THWEEEET! Now the players from both sides pushed really hard. At a score of 1 – 1,

iT WaS anyBODY'S Game.

A few minutes in and Spencer had the ball again. He soon outran Mandy Beth, Shiv and Jorge. Only

Max stood between Spencer and the goalie.

Max bent forward. His muscles tensed. He was a tiger, ready to spring.

Suddenly something colourful flicked into view. It was soaring against the clouds. Max glanced up. His mouth went dry.

There, flying directly above his head, was a giant

ORaNGe KiTe!

"Oh no!" Max gasped. Right away, he stood straight up and started doing the jumping jacks. He tried to do them quickly: one-two-three . . .

Spencer gawked at Max as he sailed past.

"NERD," he taunted.

Max was on jumping jack six when Spencer's ball clipped a planter and sailed in.

It was now 1 – 2 for Spencer's team.

By the time Max finished, all the kids had run over. The Hornets were clapping and cheering. Max's team looked at him like he was crazy. Mandy Beth was furious.

"Really, Max! Of all the times to have this happen!" she cried.

Max shrugged. He felt terrible.

"What's the game?" she asked.

He heaved a sigh. "When something flies across the sky, I've gotta do ten jumping jacks."

Shiv patted Max on the back. "It's all right, buddy," he said. "I'll tell the others that you had a leg cramp."

Mandy Beth looked up. The sky was crayon-blue. A few clouds were slowly gliding by.

"Clouds don't count," Max said. "Something has

to fly by. Like a plane."

"Like the kite," grumbled Mandy Beth.

Max hunched. *This is where I get a kick in the shin.*

BUT HE WAS WRONG.

"I guess it's not so bad. Nothin' up in the sky now," Mandy Beth said.

Just then a crow flew overhead and Max started in on the jumping jacks. "I . . . hope . . . you're . . . right," he puffed between each arm swing.

Chapter Seven

As the Crow Flies

The game was back on. Max watched from his end of the field. He was so tense he felt like an elastic band stretched to its limit.

At least the sky was clear and his jitters were **GONE.**

"C'mon Hawks!" he shouted.

All at once Max saw Shiv break through a cluster of players, the soccer ball at his feet. Shiv ran to the Hornets' net and gave the ball a good wallop.

THWACK!

The ball flew high in a perfect arc. *It skimmed Luis's fingertips and dropped in.*

Tie game: 2 – 2.

"Awesome, Shiv!" Max yelled.

We're almost there. One more goal and we're the champs, Max thought with a thrill. The Hornets only needed one goal too. But he tried not to think about that.

The whistle blew. Kids scrambled, pushed and fell. Back and forth, up and down the field.

PLAY WAS FIERCE.

Max lost track of the ball. It was trapped in a sea of shoes. Both he and Tanya were jumping and yelling, "Give it to 'em, Hawks!"

And that's when something surprising happened.

Not a woohoo-birthday-party

kind of surprise. But an oh-no-
accidentally-broke-the-living-
room-lamp kind of surprise.

From the street, a motorcycle
backfired. A loud KA-POP echoed
across the park. The noise
startled Max and Tanya. They
weren't the only ones.

CAW! CAW! CAW! In a single
sweeping wave, a flock of crows
rose out of a nearby tree.

Max saw them in the corner of
his eye.

"Don't fly this way. Don't fly this way," he begged.

But the crows could not hear him. They flew right overhead.

"One, two, three . . ." he frantically counted as the birds glided above. ". . . Eighteen, nineteen, twenty."

Max shook his head. "No, that can't be right." He quickly counted one more time as the crows became specks in the distance.

It was right! Twenty birds!

Max thought he might be sick.

Twenty birds meant

TWO HUNDRED JUMPING JACKS!

Chapter Eight

Too many JACKS

Two hundred jumping jacks!
Now what? Max panicked.

Do the jumping jacks? Then he wouldn't be able to play — for a LONG while. If I can't defend, the Hornets will score for sure.

DON'T DO THEM?

But then he'd have to tell everyone what a great player Spencer was. Sneaky, snotty Spencer Vilane.

WHAT COULD BE WORSE?

Max moaned. Two hundred might as well have been two thousand!

He peered across the field at the players. They were still clumped past midfield. Maybe he could somehow get Shiv's attention and have him call a timeout.

"One, two, three, four . . ."
Max started on the jumping jacks.
His hands slapped at his sides and
his legs kicked. Chwonk-swish,
chwonk-swish.

"Max!" cried Tanya from the
net. "What ARE you doing?"

He gave her a sorry-can't-
talk-right-now look. Then he
took off down the field. As
he ran, he did jumping jacks,
counting out loud: "Eighteen,
nineteen, twenty . . ."

Max saw the kids on the
sidelines point and holler at him.
He felt like some crazy bird that
couldn't flap hard enough to
get off the ground.

My dumb fidgets! Max thought angrily. *Why do I always get in trouble like this?*

Finally Max made it to midfield. Moving as close as possible, he hoped a player would notice him. It didn't take long.

Spitzy glanced up to locate the ball. Right away, he saw Max flapping and hopping.

"Holy moly!" he said, instantly forgetting about the game. He stopped to stare.

Jorge pushed against Spitzy, but Spitzy didn't move. Jorge looked up. Then he spotted Max too. "Max! What's goin' on?" he shouted.

Max was now doing jumping
jacks in one place. His arms
flailed wildly. His legs opened and
closed like out-of-control scissors.

"Forty-two, forty-three, forty-
four . . ."

One by one, players quit
playing. Deedee covered her
mouth in shock. Mandy Beth's
eyes bulged like they would pop
out of her head.

Max gave Shiv a desperate look. *Call a timeout, Shiv,* he willed. But Shiv was too astonished to do anything.

"Sixty-five, sixty-six, sixty-seven . . ."

Spencer was the last to realize that the game had all of a sudden come to a halt. He eyed Max and glared at the other players. No one was playing soccer anymore.

Max watched Spencer's mouth change from an angry pucker to a sly leer.

All at once, Max knew what Spencer was thinking. *Nobody was on the ball! Everyone was too busy staring at Max!*

Spencer hustled quickly to the soccer ball. Nudging it with his foot, he began to make his way around the other players. No one tried to stop him.

Max watched in horror as Spencer moved up the field.

"Eighty-three, eighty-four, eighty-five . . ."

Chapter Nine

Breakaway

With all eyes glued on Max, Spencer had a clear run upfield.

A GUARANTEED GOAL.

The Hornets would be champions!

Right away Max realized he could not stop Spencer. And he knew that Spencer saw that too. Perhaps that was why the bully was sidling up so close to Max. Like he wanted to rub the win in Max's red, puffing face. "Ninety-eight, ninety-nine. . ." wheezed Max.

"You're such a loser," Spencer sneered as he passed with the ball.

The insult hardly left Spencer's lips when, once again, something surprising happened.

Spencer had come too close to Max. As Max kicked his legs out, his right foot caught the

underside of the soccer ball.
The ball lifted and spun beyond
Spencer's reach.

It bounced twice and stopped
by Mandy Beth. Snapping out
of her trance, she pivoted then
punted.

With arms flinging and legs
sweeping, Max's eyes followed
the ball as it flew through the

air. It glided by Luis, who was too focused on Max to notice.

And it rolled right in.

Mandy Beth had scored!

Their team had won! 3 – 2.

Max's face broke out into a wide smile. He might have sounded a terrific cheer if he didn't have to keep counting.

"One hundred and eleven, one
hundred and twelve . . ."

Spencer dropped to the ground.
"Nooooo!" he howled, pounding at
the grass. His teammates shook
their heads in disbelief.

Max's team lunged at Mandy
Beth to pat her back.

"What an awesome kick!"

"You rock, Mandy Beth!"

"Way to go, girl!"

Shiv shook her hand, his face beaming.

All at once the entire Hawks team looked over at Max.

"One hundred and forty-eight, one hundred and forty-nine," Max was panting hard and his arms and legs weren't moving so well.

Players circled Max. Though they didn't know why, they started counting for him. At the two hundredth jumping jack, Max keeled over.

EVERYONE CHEERED AND CLAPPED.

Jorge doused Max with water. Shiv fell to the ground next to him, laughing.

Even Mandy Beth knelt down on the grass beside Max.

"Gee Max!" she said. "Why two hundred jumping jacks?"

"The crows . . ." Max explained between gasps. "The flock . . . of crows."

Her eyes widened. "But Max," she said, laughing. "It was a flock. ONE flock!"

"Thanks . . . Mandy Beth," he wheezed. "For telling me . . . now."

Suddenly Tanya began singing a victory song. So they all joined in. Even Max. Though he was completely out of breath.

Chapter Ten

season
Champs

"Have another, soccer champs,"
Max's mom offered.

"Thanks," said Shiv, reaching
for his second chocolate-chip
cookie.

Max, Shiv and Mandy Beth were
sitting with Mom and Granpops at

the kitchen table. Baby Sarah was in her high chair holding a sippy cup. They were all celebrating their championship win with milk and cookies. Mmm . . . mmm.

"Tell me again how you made the last goal, Mandy Beth," asked Max's grandfather.

"WHY WAS MAX AT THAT END OF THE FIELD?"

Mandy Beth shot a quick look at Max, "Well, it's sort of hard to explain . . ."

"It's like this, Granpops," interrupted Max. "I needed Shiv to call a timeout so I had to run out there to tell him."

"But why?" Granpops said.

"It was because of all the crows," answered Shiv. "There were too many of them."

"Crows?" Granpops looked confused. "What do crows have to do with a timeout in a soccer game?"

Max looked at Shiv. Shiv glanced at Mandy Beth. Mandy Beth stared back at Max.

No one knew what to say.

"My goodness, Dad," Mom spoke up, "let the kids eat. What does it matter if Max was at the wrong end of the field?"

"Well, it just doesn't make sense," Granpops said. "He's defence."

"They won," said Mom. "But more importantly, it sounds like they had a lot of fun."

"Oh yeah!" said Max, taking a bite of his cookie. "It was tons of fun."

"SO MUCH FUN,"

agreed Mandy Beth, giggling, "it made Max jump up and down."

"And flap his arms," snickered Shiv.

"About two hundred times!" Max added. He snorted so hard that milk came out of his nose.

And that made everyone at the table laugh. Even Granpops, who didn't have a clue what the three soccer champs were talking about.